The Kya Chr

Naughty Girl
By Deep

©Deep 2017

Wet N Deep Publishing

Carolyn

Enjoy the heat.

Deep

3-25-17

NAUGHTY GIRL

Dedicated to all the naughty girls.
You know who you are ... you're flipping the pages.

DEEP

Lil Girl

Ray was my dad's friend and I wanted him. Despite the twenty-year difference in our ages and the fact that he obviously had so much more experience than my twenty-year-old-self, I still wanted him.

Whenever my dad would hold poker or other card games at our house and invited his buddies over, Ray's tall hulking figure was the one I waited for to come through the door before finding something more productive to do. I looked forward to seeing his dazzling smile as he called me 'Lil Girl' before moving on to the playroom.

He was the one I would masturbate to as I heard all their voices laughing, telling vulgar jokes and the cursing being passed around, but his deep baritone voice stood out among them. The rumble of it made me cream more as my fingers fucked my tight, pink, wet pussy fast and hard as the juices slushed and ran down the inside of my thighs and onto the sheets. It was a wonder I managed to keep anyone from knowing what I was doing considering I would cum so hard to the image of him sneaking in my room and licking my pussy dry while I sucked his thick black cock.

My mom would always conveniently rush out to Aunt Mavis's house for their girls' night. Aunt Mavis's husband, Jack would be at the card games too. All of them had wives, even Ray. But when I met her, Sonya, I wondered why he was married to her. Ray's wife was a diminutive, almost mousy little thing, and definitely not pretty, with beady dark brown eyes, a big wide mouth, and washed-out looking skin.

She was not at all competition for me with the body that I've had long before it was appropriate.

My tits are heavy and round and my ass is curved and tight, my waist was small and with a slightly rounded stomach for his big hands to hold on to. My legs were long enough to wrap around him as he dicked me long and hard. My pussy was fat and puffy; perfect to cushion the pounding I wanted him to give me. I sinfully wished each night that one of these days, I would get the opportunity to show him how much of a woman ... and not a little girl ... I was and hoped it would come before I left to go upstate to college for my junior year.

Well my wish came true tonight. The get-together was cancelled. My mom wanted my dad to take her to a natural hair convention. He wasn't too happy about having to forgo his usual guys' night, but he never wanted to make my mom unhappy, so he agreed to go.

Apparently, my dad wasn't able to get in touch with everyone to cancel so he instructed me, "If Ray calls or stops by, tell him I'm sorry and I'll be in touch later to reschedule."

With an innocent daddy's girl smile, I told him, "I'll take care of it, Daddy. Have a good time."

I had a feeling Ray wouldn't be calling anyway, and I was right. Ray seemed like the type of guy that wasn't attached to devices. He showed when he showed, and left when he left.

That night, after mom and dad left, I took a shower and put on my favorite mango scented body butter before dressing in my black skintight boy shorts and a tank top that read *Juicy*. I made sure my straight long hair was out and flowing around my shoulders and put on my favorite red lip gloss that made my lips look like ripe cherries.

When the doorbell rang at eight on the dot, I took my time going to answer it. I wanted to seem unbothered and unrushed, even though I was giddy and so fuckin' horny inside. I even went through the trouble of pretending to be on my cell phone, talking to my best friend, Tiana, when I answered the door.

I opened the door with one hand, holding my phone up to my ear with the other and smiled when Ray stood there looking at me like he had been punched in the gut.

"Yeah, I know. We can always go some other time, Tiana," I said to my fake caller. "I was in the middle of getting dressed, but it won't be a big deal to come out of these clothes, so don't even sweat it."

I looked at Ray and mouthed *sorry*, as he finally picked up his bottom lip and came through the door and shut it behind him. I pretended to be listening, but I watched as he checked out my ass before I turned to him completely. He looked away quickly and started to move towards the kitchen, which led to the playroom. Now I knew I needed to hurry through my fake call.

"So hey, you go ahead and take your meds and get some sleep and call me when you get over your cold." And I quickly fake ended the call.

"Hey, sorry about that," I said to him as I followed him into the kitchen.

"No sweat," he said, but then turned back around, being sure to keep his eyes up high on my face. "Where's your dad, Lil Girl? Where's everyone else?"

"Oh, he didn't tell you? Your game night is cancelled. He went with my mom to the hair show. She begged him to go ..." I trailed off.

"Oh," he said, seeming troubled. He had no idea what trouble I could get him into if he let me.

"Yeah, he said if you wanted to hang out for a while, you could. He knows you like to get away from the house for a few hours. He thought I'd be going out anyway. But I don't mind if you stay."

He seemed even more disturbed for a moment and I hoped I hadn't pushed too far too soon.

But then he said, "Alright, I'll hang out for a little while, but not too long. I wouldn't want to bother you."

I suppose he wasn't in a rush to go home to Miss Mousy and I didn't blame him. Not when he had all of me to look at.

"Now why would you think that? I'll probably just go upstairs for a little while anyway. But do you want me to get you anything? Anything at all?" I hoped my eyes said what I was thinking. He could have anything he wanted right now. I would be putty.

"Nah, you go ahead, Lil Girl."

"One of these days you're going to stop calling me that. I'm not a little girl anymore. Can't you tell?"

I placed my hand on my curved hip, making sure he got the full picture. There was no little girl in this house. She was long gone.

Ray looked at me more fully then. It was as if he had been trying not to look at me for a long time and he'd finally been granted permission to have his fill.

His eyes trailed a hot path from my cat eyes to my lush lips, to my big tits to my hips and thighs and finally down to my legs. And then he was back to my eyes again.

"No, you aren't a little girl anymore, are you?"

My lungs could barely fill up with air. This man had made me so slick for him and all he did was look at me. My nipples became rock-hard beneath my tank top and I watched his eyes move down to them. As if sensing my arousal, his nostrils flared, before his dark brown eyes were back to looking into mine.

"But I think I'll keep calling you that for now."

Rather than blow things with him by moving too fast, too soon, I nodded and told him I'd be upstairs if he needed me for anything. He nodded real cool-like before he watched me go upstairs, but I could feel his eyes on my ass again so I made sure to allow it to shake with each deliberate step I took.

Almost an hour later, I was still alone and silently fuming in my room because he hadn't said a peep to me. I thought he might have fallen asleep, since it was so quiet downstairs and since my parents would only be gone for another two hours, I was running out of time. Right when I was going to go check on him, I heard movement out in the hallway and then the sound of the bathroom door closing.

That's odd, I thought.

There's a guest bathroom downstairs so Ray could have easily used that one, but didn't. A few moments later, the bathroom door creaked open and his footsteps could be heard again but only this time, they were moving towards my bedroom.

And then he was standing there in my doorway looking at me like he wanted to eat me and I definitely wanted him to.

"Whatchu doin'?" He asked me.

God I loved his voice. It was deep and perfect.

"Waiting."

"Waiting for what?" He wanted to know.

"For you."

At this, he just nodded.

"I figured as much. How long you been waiting?"

"For a couple of years," I responded breathlessly. I opened my thighs to make myself clear, not that I thought I needed to, at this point.

"So have I." He admitted, eyeing my fabric-covered snatch.

I was now panting and so damn wet, all he had to do was pull his dick out and slide into me and we could get it over with.

"So what are you waiting for?" Now I was too high on my lust to care how bold I had gotten.

"Take off your shorts," he ordered.

I hurried to do as he said, pulling them off quickly, not at all embarrassed by how wet I was and how obvious it was as I slid off the cotton shorts.

I'd been wanting to be fucked by this man since I was sixteen and the moment was here. He grabbed the shorts and inspected them, sniffing the scent of them before trailing his tongue along the glistening and sticky seam.

"Mmmmn. You have a wet pussy, huh?"

"For you, yes."

"We'll see."

"I want you to."

"Take off your tank ... slowly. I want to see those big tits bounce as you do it."

Again, I did as he asked, making sure to move slowly enough that he had the full effect of my triple Ds jiggling and shaking with my movements.

"Pretty fuckin' tits," he praised, making me squirm.

Now he was rubbing his hard cock through his black jeans as he was watching me and it was too damn erotic for me to just sit there. I know he didn't tell me to, but I couldn't resist.

I got off of the bed and moved to squat down in front of him. I hurried to unbuckle his jeans. He had on no underwear so it took no time to release him from the fabric and take him in my mouth.

I made quick work of getting his thick cock to the back of my throat, not caring if I gagged. I had no idea when or if I could taste him again, so I gorged myself on him ... licking, bobbing, choking and slobbing.

Soon his hands grabbed my face and he fucked my mouth while chanting, "Good Lil Girl."

I loved it.

It fucking turned me on; so much so that I reached down to rub my fat clit and begin to fuck myself with my small fingers as I brought him to a nut. I swallowed his thick warm cum as he shouted out, his grip on my head was nearly painful.

After a few moments, he ordered me back on the bed and I followed his order. I laid there and watched as he finished undressing, revealing smooth, chocolate brown skin and strong muscles.

"Are you on birth control?" he asked while stroking his dick back to an erection.

"I am. I promise," I told him.

"Good."

And then he was on top of me. In one fluid motion, he was inside of me. Stretching me, going deeper than I imagined. My hips rose to meet his demanding thrusts, enjoying the savage way he was taking me.

"Damn, you're tight, Lil Girl," he groaned.

"And you're so fucking big," I gasped. "But don't you fucking stop," I hurried to say when he slowed down.

He fucked me so good and so hard I swore we were two seconds away from breaking the bed before he asked me to get down on the floor on my knees. His big body came behind mine and entered me so hard I nearly cracked a tooth. It would have been worth it though.

Our skin slapped against each other as I worked back against his, encouraged by his hands on my waist pulling me back toward him. Ray spanking my jiggling ass only made me work harder. He reached around me, grabbing one of my swinging breasts and tweaking the nipple as his other hand reached between my thighs. Ray's finger circled around my clit, making my sopping cunt clench tightly around him in spasms.

I cried out, as I lost track of my rhythm and my mind, and I would have collapsed if he hadn't been holding me as he shot his load inside of me.

In the moments that followed, we kissed quickly, he held me, and then hurried me to the bathroom to take a shower with him where he finger fucked me as I gave him a hand job.

Once we were clean, he dressed and then went downstairs just in case someone came home and waited for me to come down to see him out.

At the door, he brushed a kiss against my lips, slowly and softly.

"I won't tell a soul," I promised him.

"I know you won't. Not if you want more. And I know you do," he said, and then he was gone.

No one would hear a word of this because I definitely wanted more.

NAUGHTY GIRL

The Best of Friends

Tiana and I were tight, and had been that way since attending the same day camp together. We were the kind of friends that hung out and did dumb shit, nothing at all productive. We smoked a little weed, went to clubs; that kinda thing. But Tiana mentally wasn't going to the same kind of places I was going. I planned to have a real job one day, the kind of job that would make me some real cash. Tiana, well, she worked wherever she could, but our different paths didn't matter to me, we were still tight.

While I was in my junior year at the University of Chester, I would only see her when I could get home. School was about an hour away, so about once a month when I needed to get some money from my folks and to fuck Ray, I would come home.

Ray and I were cool. We fucked and that was it. Though there were times we did other things like watching TV after sex, but he'd always have to leave the hotel room we rented so that he could go back to his ugly wife. Anyway, his dick was good and I didn't plan to stop having it, so whatever.

Anyway, one particular weekend, I came home and Ray was acting funny, like he couldn't meet up with me. He said his wife had plans for them. I noticed that he had to deal with that a lot lately. Like she knew her husband was giving up that dick elsewhere and she was trying to hold on tighter by signing them up for shit he really didn't want to do, but to not hear her mouth, he did it.

I would claim that I didn't care, but deep down, he pissed me off. I wanted to tell her to give it up. All that shit wasn't going to stop his fucking around, but it *would* make me mad.

So he wasn't available and Tiana was, so I hooked up with her. We went to Club Passion and drank our asses off and danced. After a while, I forgot all about missing out on Ray's good dick. He could spend all the time in the world with his mousy wife.

I remembered the last time I was here. It was a couple of months ago, and I had met this sexy muthafucka. My favorite time at the club was at the end of the night because at that point, I would know whether I'd be going home alone to my extensive collection of bells and whistles that would have me creaming and wanting to scream so hard that I'd risk waking my folks up. Or it could end like that night a couple of months ago, when the right muthafucka approached me, talked good enough game, and seemed okay enough to replace my vibrator for the night and I went home with him.

Out on the dance floor, sexy muthafucka of the night and I were bumping and grinding to 2Pac's, *How Do You Want It*, before he leaned in and said, "How do *you* want it?"

I grabbed his dick and realized I wanted him every which way as long as he put it in me nice and deep.

"I want it deep," I told him.

"Bet," was his response.

"Let's go now," I told him.

I had always been into older men anywhere from just a few years and most recently as much as twenty years, but there was also this thing I liked about them when they were this young. There wasn't that power struggle or the laziness you got with older men set in their ways and wanting you to do all the damn work. Nah, these puppies came when I snapped.

Twenty minutes later, we were at a cheap but clean hotel, and I was on him. "Slow down, Ma," he called me that because I hadn't seen the need to tell him my name and he never asked. "We've got all night," he pleaded with me as I ripped his clothes off of him, one piece at a time.

As I pulled my T-shirt dress over my head, allowing my tits to swing and bounce free, my already hardened dark-brown nipples had him changing his mind.

"Maybe you're right. We've been taking it slow all night. Now is not the time for slow."

He watched me with a smirk, but his hard length wasn't smiling. In fact, it looked angry, hard and so erect that the bronzed-brown skin was stretched so tight that with one wrong move, it would be all over.

I laughed a little. "I tell you what?"

"What?"

"Why don't you freshen up a little at the sink," I said, and turned around to walk to the bathroom.

It's not like I planned to put his feet in my mouth. All I needed was his dick.

"I'm going to take a quick shower." I could feel his eyes on my ass, so I made it bounce for him and closed the bathroom door before reopening it to tell him, "Wait for me in the bed."

Anyway, after washing under the spray of the hot water, I left out of the bathroom and was greeted with him lying butt ass naked on top of the covers, playing with his phone.

Probably texting his girl with some lie about where he was at the moment.

I came over to the bed and joined him, placing a rubber on his dick. I slid my body up his, kissing him once on his lips before I slid this pussy down on that dick and rode him hard and fast. Getting off more from that slapping sound of skin to skin, the staccato of our heavy breaths pushing out through our opened lips.

My feet planted onto the mattress, sheets in disarray, his toes curling as I worked and jerked and made his body weep into the rubber. After cumming hard and collapsing next to him, I said, "Now we take it slow."

But he must have had a change of mind. "Fuck that," he said with enough aggression that made me wetter. He positioned himself between my legs and I grabbed his head as he lowered himself to my pussy. I pumped my clit against his face, forcing him to take me with his lips and his tongue. His fingers then worked inside of me against my spot, curling just right, making me squirt into his mouth.

He lapped it up between my wet thighs before forcing my legs behind my ears and sliding into me so hard I bit my damn tongue. You know when you think you might be about to lose your uterus for a moment and you place your hand against his hip like, *wait a minute ... stop?*

Yeah, that's where I was.

But he didn't stop; he pounded me so good, that when he was done, I just waved at him as he left me curled up on the bed, with my thumb in my mouth.

Yeah, I remember that night.

But it didn't look like I would have that kind of luck tonight. Just as we were leaving out though, Tiana said she saw Donny.

I was like, "Who's Donny?"

"Oh, he's the guy I've been seeing for about three months now. I thought I told you about him."

This is when I realized she must have really liked Donny because she didn't want me to meet him. See, Tiana was a bit insecure when it came to me. She knew it and so did I. When guys approached me and not her, she automatically thought it was because I was prettier. I don't necessarily think that's true. Tiana is beautiful and her body is banging. I think there is just something about me that guys liked. They also just happen to be the guys that she liked. So I get it.

You don't want your man 'round me; I don't blame you.

We finally made it over to Donny, who was ordering a drink. When he turned around, drink in hand, he noticed me first. Donny smiled wide and was about to say something to me when he noticed Tiana was standing beside me.

The smile on his face changed a little, but he reached out to grab her, drink sloshing on the floor in front of him and barely missing my bared toes.

"Hey, Boo. Didn't know you were coming out."

"I hadn't planned on it," Tiana said. "You know I have to clock in at eight at the grocery store, but since my girl is back in town, I made an exception."

It was then that Donny allowed himself to look at me again since it was now appropriate to. His appraisal was swift, but there was enough heat there that my pussy felt it.

Introductions were made and I politely shook his hand. He was cute; cuter than I was used to Tiana being with. He was more my type, six feet two inches, milk-chocolate skin. Nice white teeth and trimmed goatee. He was more than cute, he was fine and if he wasn't holding Tiana so tight, I might have wanted to fuck him.

"I've heard Tiana mention you. Seems I get to meet the mysterious and studious, Kya."

"Seems so." I wouldn't say much more or I know Tiana would trip. But right then, Tiana covered her mouth.

"What's wrong?" Her man asked.

Before she could answer him, Tiana ran towards the bathroom area, which told me she was sick.

"I'll go check on her," I told him.

Tiana *was* sick; too much drinking I guess. Once I helped get her cleaned up after she threw up a couple of times in that nasty ass bathroom stall, we came out of the bathroom to find Donny waiting.

"I'll take her home with me," he said.

"Oh, okay." I was kind of in a hurry to get home to my dildo anyway.

"But why don't you come with us? That way you're there when she wakes up. I might have to leave out early and don't want her to be alone," he said.

"Sure."

So we left.

He gave me his address, which I plugged into my navigational system and I followed him to his spot. I helped him get her up to the second-floor apartment and waited in his sparsely furnished living room while he got her in bed.

His place was small but neat. The colors were inviting, making me wonder if Tiana helped him decorate but nah, they hadn't been together long enough.

"You want something to drink?" He asked me once he returned. His eyes were intense and hot, and they made it clear that he wanted me. I knew it, which is why I accepted his offer to come back to his place knowing good and well he didn't need to leave early.

"Yes, water, please. We did a little bit of drinking. I need to flush it out."

"So who was going to drive home?" He asked this as he headed to his small kitchenette where I followed him.

"Me. I'm fine really, but Tiana went a bit too far."

"Yeah, she tends to do that sometimes," he said, and I wondered what he was talking about.

He handed me the water and our fingers brushed, but I ignored it since he'd have to be the one to make a move to cheat on his girl, even if she was my girl too. I opened the bottle and drank from it while he watched me.

"So, do you smoke?" He asked.

"Yeah, a little. Not as much while I'm in school."

"Cool. You wanna do some with me?"

"Sure."

I don't know, maybe he thought that he would have to get me fucked up to get this pussy, but that was so not the case here.

"Come on," he said, and led me into the living room.

We sat down on his couch and I watched him pull out a little pipe and said that since he knew I'd have to get going at some point, we'd do the one hitter so it wouldn't fuck me up like smoking a blunt would. That confirmed it; he didn't need to leave early.

We sat there and did a couple of bowls. I was floating away and so relaxed that I barely felt that I was in my body and he was sitting next to me, probably feeling the same way. The state I was in probably made it easy for him to have me undressed and pinned to the couch without me realizing it. But I was completely aware that what we were doing was wrong, but I kissed his mouth anyway. I also let him slob me down like I was his woman, and like his woman wasn't in the other room knocked out; like she wasn't my best friend who would be crushed by what I was about to do to her fine ass man.

When he took my tight nipples into his mouth, I arched and held his head close to me, encouraging him to play with them the way I liked it and damn it, how I needed since Ray's ass was fucking around.

They were hard and wet when he blew on them and I started to unzip his jeans and he bit one gently before flicking it. Donny had a big, thick, long, hard and hot dick and I wanted to suck him off. I got on my knees, still on the couch, and leaned over to take him deep in my throat as he sat back to enjoy the blowjob.

After a while, he leaned forward, reaching around and behind me, fingering my pussy, rubbing his thumb across and around my wet bud. He started to fuck me hard with his fingers, stretching my walls to prepare me for him. He had three of his fingers inside of me and I was working myself back against them and I still needed more.

My thighs were slick and coated with my juices and it was clear that I was more than ready to fuck, but I wanted him to taste me. I let go of his dick and got up to sit on the back of the couch and leaned back against the white plaster wall before I parted my thighs.

"Eat it," I commanded.

He got between my legs, pushed apart my fat lips and lapped me up like I was sweet and he had a sweet tooth. Sucking on my pussy as I grabbed his head and held it to me as I rubbed against his lips. He was so damn good. No wonder Tiana was keeping him a secret.

I pushed myself against his greedy mouth and creamed silently when he inserted a finger and curled it against my G-spot.

He sat down on the couch, grabbed a rubber and covered himself and I immediately straddled him, sliding down on his dick, crying out when he stretched me. I didn't hesitate to bounce up and down on his dick.

My tits were smacking his jaws as he leaned in and placed his face in between them. His hands grabbed my jiggling ass as he thrust up to meet each of my down strokes. In rhythm, we were perfection. This shit was hot and just the thought of it made me ripple around him in a rush. We both started to come and he smothered my screams with his mouth.

We did it a few times that night; once on his kitchen counter and again on his living room floor. We also did it once in the bathroom with him fucking me from behind while we watched each other in the mirror, turned on more by the sight of the shit we were doing to each other.

"I'm going to get going. Make sure she is okay after I go," I told him.

He kissed me one last time before walking me out to my car and waiting until I drove off.

Tiana called me later that day, sounding like she was still a little green around the gills, and asked me what happened last night as if Donny hadn't given her some lie. I told her she got sick and Donny took her home with him. I told her I left so that she could get some rest.

She and Donny stayed together a few months after that and during that time; he came up to my school to visit. We fucked when he came and that was it. We never talked about what we were doing or where it would go and we never talked about Tiana. Besides, I still had Ray, who was wondering why I didn't come home as often.

NAUGHTY GIRL

Blackjack

I love masturbating and it loves me. Sometimes I think it's the best sex I ever had. I say that because the best and most intense orgasms that I've had, I've had by myself. I'm talking about orgasms that made my heart pound and my head hurt when I'm through.

Don't get me wrong, I love fucking. I absolutely love me some dick, specifically big dick. The feel of it in my hand, the taste of it in my mouth, and not to mention feeling the warmth of it inside me. But, not having a man around has never stopped me from cumming like a maniac. There have been days where I've spent the day doing nothing but masturbating, sleeping, watching TV and eating. Today was going to be one of those days.

Since I didn't have any classes on Fridays, I drove home on Thursday after my last class. After stopping by the house to do laundry and get some cash, I told my folks that I was going back to school to study for an English test on Monday.

After my last paper, my professor, Ms. Angela Gram was talking about failing me if I didn't start doing the work that she knew I was capable of producing. I was a straight A student, had been all my life, so the fact that this woman had let the words, *I'm going to fail you, Kya,* come flying out of her mouth was totally unacceptable.

But instead of packing up and heading back to my dorm to study, I drove to the Doubletree Hotel, had a couple of drinks at the bar and then I called Ray.

"I'm at the Crowne Plaza, naked, wet and waiting for you to come fuck me."

"I understand that, Keenen." I know when he calls me Keenen that he is with Mousy. "And as much as I'd like to come help you out with that, Sonya and I are at her favorite restaurant and then we're going to take in a movie," Ray said over my laughter.

"Okay then, I tell you what, tell me what restaurant you're at and I'll call you when I'm in the parking lot," I said.

"Really, why is that?"

"So you can come outside, bend me over and give me that dick and then you can go back inside and be a good husband."

"You know that sounds like a good idea, but I don't think I'm going to be able to do that. But if something happens to change that, Keenen, I'll be sure to call. But I want you to understand that I really do hate to miss out on that." And then I heard Mousy asking him what was taking so long.

"Yeah, I bet you do," I said, ended the call and then I called Donny. He came right over, but since he had a date with his new girlfriend, it was just a quickie that left me wanting more.

Now this may come as some surprise, but as much as I like to fuck and get fucked, with the exception to the occasional club hook-up, I won't fuck just anybody. As of right now, it was just Ray and Donny that I allowed between my thighs, so once Donny left and Ray didn't call, I was left alone and frustrated, so I went to sleep.

When I woke up the next morning, it wasn't even six o'clock yet, but my pussy was already wet, my clit was plump and my lips felt swollen. When my pussy is ripe like that, it gets puffy. My lips move farther apart, my slit opens some and I could feel myself creaming on top of the sheets. She was warm, empty and ready to get fucked. I needed something to make me cum.

Once I did what I needed to do in the bathroom, I got back in bed. I reached in the nightstand, took out my nasty bag of tricks and pulled out Blackjack. It was called *The Fifty Shades Greedy Girl G-Spot Rabbit Vibrator* and I sometimes referred to him as Jack. It promised that its thirty-six possible vibration mode combinations would deliver incredible orgasms and they weren't fucking lying about that shit.

It was black, long, sleek, and curved just right with enough girth to pummel my wet walls with precision while knocking on my spot. Blackjack did exactly what I needed him to do and I gotta be honest, I never leave home without him. Then I took out my glass crystal ball anal plug and even though my juices were slowly seeping into my ass, I got out some coconut oil.

Once I had sufficiently lubricated my ass, I slowly inserted the crystal ball, relaxed and laid back on the bed. I spread my legs and reached for Jack. When I did that, it seemed as if my lips opened to accept him. I slid him inside of me slowly, allowed him to fill me up and then I exhaled. I began sliding it in and out of me while I gently squeezed my nipple. As I fucked myself slowly, I thought about Ray.

One night when we were together, I told him that I wanted him to fuck me in my ass. But no matter how long and hard we tried that night; his dick was just too big for my virgin opening. I felt bad, but not Ray; he just laughed a little and then he tongued my asshole.

"We just gonna have to train that fat juicy ass to take this dick, Lil Girl."

Ray and I had experimented with a starter anal plug that was sexy and shaped like a spade. For some reason, which I can't really explain, the fact that it was glass was intimidating at first. But when I placed the cool bulb at my puckered hole, I relaxed. It felt good and then it was stretching me.

Since I really wanted Ray to be the one to open my ass up, I started putting the anal plug in my ass when I was masturbating. At first, it felt weird, full, almost uncomfortable, but at the same time, it was very arousing.

The thought of Ray fucking me and the feeling of that plug in there was enough to make me increase my pace. Before long, I was plunging Blackjack in and out of me so hard and so fast that I felt my orgasm building quickly.

In my mind, I could see Ray above me, my legs were wrapped around his waist and he is the one fucking the shit outta me. The explosion that wracked my body made me shudder and shake as I screamed loud and long. My body contorted and a light sheen of sweat covered me where I lay.

I lie there, breathing hard and trembling with Blackjack and the spade still lodged inside me. I laid still and quiet for a while, trying to compose myself, but every time I thought about Ray fucking me and the intense orgasm I just brought myself to, my thighs would press together, my pussy would clench and I would cum again. When my heartbeat slowed and my breathing returned to some semblance of normalcy, I placed the rabbit ears on my engorged bud and turned Blackjack on.

Even though Blackjack had the thirty-six possible vibration mode combinations, there were three that were my 'go to' settings. I had a name for each setting combination and used them depending on how I wanted to cum.

There was slow love, master blaster and pure insanity. I set Blackjack to master blaster, pressed my thighs together and held it in place because I love it like that. For one, it's the length of the stimulation. There is pressure from the vibrator as it's rubbing against my G-spot, while the rabbit is stimulating my clit and it feels like I'm having two orgasms. I'm always afraid of it at first, because it seems like too much energy is getting ready to combust. But when I let go, it's the greatest rush.

The sensation radiated throughout my entire body until every muscle in my body seemed to lock and my pussy began clenching and releasing around Blackjack. My eyes rolled back in their sockets, my mouth opened wide and I came and squirted so hard that my walls tightened and Blackjack blasted out of my pussy. Once I had calmed down and could think straight, I took the anal plug out, cleaned and put away my toys. Since the sheets were wet, I got in the other bed and went back to sleep.

When I woke up later that morning, I was hungry. Since it wasn't nine yet, I got out of bed, took a shower, put some clothes on, and went to the lobby to have breakfast.

While I dined on spicy sausage, eggs and roasted potatoes, I eyed the cutie who was there having breakfast with his wife and their three badass kids. At first, they were annoying, running around and getting into everything, but after a while, the parents got them settled down to eat and then it became funny to watch. All the while he was having problems, he was making eye contact with me and smiling. When he got up to leave with his loud ass family, I blew him a kiss and mouthed the words, *have fun*.

After finishing my juice, I got up and went back to my room, got undressed and got back in the bed. It didn't take long before I was fingering myself to the thought of breakfast cutie, without the wife and kids of course, taking me from behind while I leaned against the breakfast bar.

As promised, I spent the entire day masturbating and sleeping, called for Chinese delivery, fucked myself and went back to sleep. It wasn't until late in the afternoon, when Tiana called and said that she was going to swing by and pick me up.

"What we gonna do?" I asked.

"Me and Donny were just gonna hangout at his place, have some drinks and get blazed. So, I was thinking that me and you could go get something to eat and then we shoot over to Donny's," Tiana said, and I was a bit surprised. Especially since the night before, he told me that he wasn't seeing her anymore.

At first I said, "That's all right. I'll get with you tomorrow," because I really wasn't feeling hanging out with her and Donny.

I had planned on not fucking Donny anymore. One, because there were times, like last night, when he would cum too quick and leave me wet and wanting. And two, he was my best friend's man, she was all into him and it was just plain wrong. Yes, I may have fucked him but I never wanted to hurt her; and she would be if she found out.

As discreetly as I could, I tried to let my girl know that he was no good, but she wasn't trying to hear none of that shit. The boy definitely had skills when he was on his game, so if he was putting it on her like he had put it on me, I couldn't blame her.

But Tiana wouldn't take no for an answer, so I said come on. She said that she would be here in an hour, but knowing her like I do, I knew that it would be more like an hour and a half.

"Plenty of time."

I set Blackjack for pure insanity and went for it. After I came for the fifth time that day, I dragged myself out of bed, took a shower and got dressed. I put on my favorite black dress with no panties, and was ready when Tiana got there.

"Hey, Kya."

"Hey, girl," I said as I opened the door, surprised when I saw Donny was with her.

"What's up, Kya," Donny said, and ran his tongue over his lips.

"I was thinking that instead of going to Donny's place that we could just hang out here," Tiana said.

"That's cool, but I would still like to get something to eat," I said. *Cumming all day makes you hungry*, I thought to myself.

"Yeah, we can do that," Donny said, and licked his lips again.

"Cool. Let me get my purse and we can go."

"Let me use your bathroom," Tiana said.

"Sure."

Once Tiana was in the bathroom and had closed the door, Donny stepped to me quickly. He pulled me to his chest and tried to penetrate me with his finger.

"Stop," I said, and pushed him off me. "Tiana is in the next room."

"So, it wouldn't be the first time," he said, and grabbed me again.

"I know," I said softly, and pushed him off again. "But this time she is not passed out drunk," *asshole*. I heard the toilet flush. "See, she'll be out in a second."

When Tiana came out of the bathroom, we left my room and Donny took us to dinner at the Olive Garden. Over dinner, Donny was openly flirting with me. Now, I may have a low moral compass when it comes to sex, I mean I am fucking my best friend's man, but him flirting with me in front of her face was just flat out disrespectful. It reinforced my decision never to let him see this pussy again.

After we finished eating, we rolled by the liquor store and then we headed for the room. So there we are, having a good time drinking and smoking weed, when out of nowhere, Donny starts flirting with me again.

I mean dude was actually trying to talk up a threesome on the low and I can tell that it's making Tiana uncomfortable. I was about to tell them I was tired and ask them to leave when my phone rang.

When I looked at the display and saw that it was Ray calling, my kitty cat immediately started to throb.

"Hello."

"What's up, Lil Girl? You still at the Crowne?"

"I sure am."

"Which one?"

"The one on Grand and Lance."

"Good. What room you in?"

"Three twenty-seven. Why?"

"I don't have a lot of time, and I'm not far from there, so I was gonna swing by there for a few."

Really?

A fuckin' quickie?

Really?

First no dick at all, and then a fuckin' quickie?

I glanced over at last night's quickie who was still eyeing me like his girl wasn't watching and thought about how I didn't want to spend another night alone, wet and frustrated. I wanted Ray to come over here and take his time fucking me until my eyes rolled back in my head and I screamed at the top of my lungs, 'I can't take no more!'

"I'm busy right now."

"Doing what?"

"Just sitting around with some friends."

"Okay," Ray said. "I'll call you later."

"Okay," I said, and ended the call, hoping that when he called back, he'd be calling with something stronger than 'I don't have a lot of time'.

While I was on the phone with Ray, Tiana had made us both another drink, I guess to calm her nerves, and Donny had sparked up another blunt. While I listened to them talk about some shit I didn't want to hear about, I looked at the nightstand that had my nasty bag of tricks and thought about what I was going to use on myself the minute Tiana and Donny left. I was fantasizing about fucking myself with the big brown dildo I called Mandingo, when my phone rang. I looked at the display and once again, it was Ray.

"What's up?"

"Come outside, I got something for you," Ray said, and ended the call. The fact that he was outside made my walls clench. I stood up, stepped into my heels and had my hand on the doorknob before I said, "I'll be right back," and I was out the door.

When I got outside, I looked around the parking lot for Ray's car. It was dark, so it took me a minute, but I finally spotted it backed in at the far end of the parking lot surrounded by a lot of brush, and I began walking toward it. I didn't see Ray, and it wasn't until I got closer that I saw that the trunk was opened and that's probably where he was.

"Hey, Ray," I said when I was close enough for him to hear me. "What you got for me?"

"Come back here and see, Lil Girl."

When I got behind the car, Ray was standing there and he was stroking that fat black juicy dick in his hand.

"Is that what you got for me?"

"It is."

"How did you know that was what I wanted?"

"Because you always want this dick, and I always want to give it to you," Ray said, as I squatted down and took him into my mouth. I loved having Ray in my mouth and I loved the way his dick tasted as I worked it deeper down my throat.

I'd been working on relaxing the muscles in my throat so I could take more of him in without gagging, so when Ray grabbed my head with both of his massive hands and started fucking my mouth, I was ready.

"Damn, girl," Ray breathed out and I looked up to watch the way his eyes rolled back in their sockets as I pulled him deeper into my hot mouth. I felt it expand in my mouth and I got ready to swallow each and every drop, but Ray suddenly jerked his dick out of my mouth and stepped back quickly.

I smiled.

He stood there for a moment stroking that dick before he said, "Take off that dress."

"What?"

"I said come outta that fuckin' dress," Ray ordered, and I quickly pulled the dress over my head and slung it in the trunk. I just stood there in front of Ray in nothing but my heels and a bra while he stroked his dick.

"The bra too."

I spun around. "Unhook me," I ordered and he quickly complied. I slid the straps off my shoulders and let my bra fall in the trunk.

Ray gently placed one hand on my back and the other on my hip and bent me over gently. I placed my hands in the trunk as Ray rubbed the head of his dick up and down my moist lips before he entered me slowly, inch by delicious inch, until his entire length was inside me.

"This pussy feels so fuckin' good, Lil Girl," Ray said, and grinded that dick into me. That shit felt so fuckin' good, so fuckin' warm, so fuckin' hard and my pussy began snatching and releasing around him.

Ray started out fucking me slowly, in and out leisurely, squeezing my swinging tits and fingering my clit like we had all the time in the world and we weren't in the Crowne Plaza's parking lot.

And despite the high I was on having him handle me this way, the way I wanted all day, I knew this was not the place to have an all-out fuck session. Then Ray began pounding away like both of those facts suddenly became apparent to him and he had to go ahead and bust a nut quickly.

Well, Ray being Ray, he pounded away at this pussy for a good ten minutes, during which time, I came twice on that dick before I felt it expand like a log and he exploded inside of me.

We stood there for a while; Ray had all but collapsed on my back. His hands were full of my tits and he was still rock hard inside me.

"Get rid of your friends and I'll be back a little after midnight," he whispered in my ear before he straightened up and eased out of me.

Once I made him shiver by sucking my juices off him, we both got dressed. He left and I waddled back in the room, put Tiana and Donny out so I could masturbate over the incredible fucking Ray just put on me.

NAUGHTY GIRL

Extra Credit

After I put Tiana and Donny out, I came hard with Blackjack. Yes, I can come all day if I want to, but usually it puts me in a good sleep. It was after two in the morning when Ray finally got back to my room and knocked on the door. I got out of bed and went to let him in.

"What took you so long?" I asked, and headed back to the bed, sliding beneath the warm covers.

"I had some things to take care of," he said, which meant he had to appease his Mousy wife. If that was supposed to bother me, it didn't, especially when he was walking towards the bed, naked and very ready. All I cared about was him being inside of me.

Ray knelt at the edge of the bed and began stroking his dick. "Play with yourself, Lil girl." I began to reach for Blackjack. "No," he barked and I froze. "Just use your hands."

I ran my hands slowly across my tits and squeezed them, while my eyes were glued to the sight of Ray cupping his balls and gliding his hand up and down his dark hard wood.

"Shake them for me," he told me and moved a little closer. "I like watching you shake those pretty titties."

"I like shaking them for you."

"Squeeze your nipples."

Since they were aching to be touched, I did so quickly.

Ray brought that dick a little closer. He was squeezing his nipple and stroking that fat dick faster and I wondered if he was going to make himself cum and shoot his juices all over me.

"Take one in your mouth and suck it."

The second my lips got wrapped around my nipple, Ray leaned in and slowly ran his tongue up my slit. He lingered at my clit and got it wet while he continued to stroke himself. With his dick still in his hand, Ray moved around the bed beside me. "Play with your clit."

I let go of my nipple and let the other fall out of my mouth. As I spread my lips and began circling on my clit, Ray eased one of my nipples back in my mouth.

"Suck it."

Us getting off on each other was so damn hot and erotic, I was close to cumming but trying to hold off to make it more intense.

Ray let go of my tit and once again, it fell out of my mouth. "Put two fingers in and fuck yourself," he ordered and eased his dick in my mouth.

I tasted him, slobbing, bobbing, licking and sucking every bit of dick I could get my lips around. I got so turned on that I began ramming my fingers into my now drenched body.

I was close to cumming and Ray must have known it, because he grabbed my head and fucked my mouth until I came. I had to literally spit his dick out of my mouth so I could scream.

While I lay on the bed shuttering, shaking and mumbling incoherently about wanting that dick, Ray laughed and got up from the bed. He stood there for a while, stroking that big fuckin' cock and looking at me.

"Get on your knees and turn around."

I quickly scooted toward him and got on my knees. "You gonna fuck me in my ass now?"

Ray slapped it once. "I'll have that ass, when I'm ready for that ass, Lil Girl," he said, and slammed his dick into my wet and wanting pussy. While he plunged deeper inside me, Ray placed his hand on my back making me arch more into the bed so that my face was pressed against my cum-drenched sheets.

Ray fucked me long, hard and in a variety of positions until I felt him expanding inside me, like earlier, but rather than waste it, I planned to swallow. I quickly moved to turn to him and took him into my wanting mouth and sucked his dick until his muscles locked, his eyes and mouth opened wide and he came so fuckin' hard in my mouth that I could barely swallow all of his cum without gagging on it.

We both collapsed on the bed, lying there for a while in silence. I snuggled up close to Ray and he put his arm around me. After a while in our silence, I began stroking his cock. Once it was hard again, I started sucking it and before long, I was on top of him, riding him with the skill I had perfected since being with him.

None of that rubbing and grinding, not unless he just wanted to watch me get off, which he loved too. But when he wanted me to take him there, I planted my feet on top of the mattress, and with my long legs, I squatted over him to take his dick inside of my wet cunt. Working myself up and down on his thick dick with powerful movements so all he felt was this pussy swallowing him up and retreating.

See, Ray liked to 'feel all of this pussy' when I was on top, but prior to him, riding dick never really got me off so it wasn't like I would run to jump on it. I always thought it was because of my height; my long legs preventing me from being in the right position for enjoyment, but he taught me how to make good use of my legs.

It was five o'clock when Ray announced that he had to go home so he could be there when Mousy woke up, but he promised that he would be back in a couple of hours.

"So get some rest, Lil Girl, 'cause I plan on fuckin' you all day when I get back," Ray said, and closed the door behind him.

"Promises, promises," I said to him and headed for the shower.

Hours later, while I was asleep, I was awakened by a loud knocking on the door. "Housekeeping!" the female attendant yelled, and that was when I realized that I forgot to put the do not disturb sign on the door.

"Just a minute!" I yelled back and looked at the clock. I put on another T-shirt dress, this time in blue, and stepped into my heels, thinking that I would go eat something while she cleaned the room.

When I got back to the room an hour later, the room was clean and much to my surprise, when I stepped out onto the balcony, Ray's car was in the parking lot below. He knocked on the door a few minutes later.

"Didn't think I was coming back, did you?" Ray said and followed me into the room.

"No, not really. I figured you'd be with your wife today. But I'm glad you came back," I said, and pulled the dress over my head to reveal my naked body.

Ray kept his promise and fucked me for the rest of the day until he went home to Mousy. But before he left, he gave me what I'd been dying for.

Ray had been lying between my thighs for the last hour, licking, sucking, nibbling, and fingering my pussy bringing me to multiple orgasms. I was dripping wet, as were the sheets beneath me. He got to his knees and grabbed one of the pillows.

"Arch your back," he ordered, and slid the pillow under my ass. Then he lifted my legs and entered me.

He fucked me hard, deep, and fast, you know, the way I love for him to and I came hard on his dick. But instead of forcing his dick in my mouth and letting me taste myself, Ray pulled out, stuck three of his fingers in and finger fucked me. After a few deep strokes, he pulled his fingers out and ran his wet finger around and in my ass.

My body began shaking with anticipation as Ray allowed his spit to drizzle down from his lip. I felt the warmth of it fall onto my pussy and down into my ass. Ray eased his fingers in and out of me and rubbed the wetness on the head of his dick.

"Give it to me, Ray. Don't make me wait anymore."

Ray slapped my thigh. "I'll have that ass, when I'm ready for that ass, Kya," he said again, but this time instead of slamming his dick into my wet and wanting pussy, Ray gently placed the tip of his dick against my waiting and wanting ass, letting me know he was now ready.

He eased the head in and then Ray slowly began to push it in slowly, little by little. The pressure was intense and at first, my body wanted to reject the invasion until he encouraged me to 'relax and take it'. I did relax and after a while, he was able to get enough in to slide back and forth inside of me. It was still pretty tight and I felt filled up so I didn't do much moving, but when he began to toy with all my buttons, my nipples and my clit, I forgot how uncomfortable I felt and enjoyed it.

Ray told me I was opening up more and he started to move faster inside of me. For the first time, I felt a different kind of pressure and though I wasn't sure what would happen next, I relaxed and let it happen. This explosion was different. It was so consuming, so scary that I almost cried. Not cry out, but cry as in boohoo tears. But I managed to hold it in.

Ray pulled out and shot his hot cum all over my stomach. We took a shower before he got me back into bed and held me for a while, and then he left.

I slept like a baby after Ray left and in the morning, I got up early, got my stuff packed, and had breakfast before making the drive back to college. I had an English test the following day and I really needed to study.

As I drove, I took a minute to consider the fact that, instead of spending the weekend to study for what has become the most important test of my college career; I was laid up in a hotel getting my brains fucked out by Ray and his magnificent dick and tongue.

Although it seemed worth it at the time, now, in retrospect, I probably should have brought my horny ass back here on Friday afternoon. The proof of that came on Wednesday when I got my test paper back.

"D!"

She gave me a fuckin' D? I've never gotten a fuckin' D in my entire life! I wanted to march right up there, shove that paper in her face and say, "What the fuck you mean giving me a D!" But I didn't. I sat there like a good girl and waited until class was over and everybody else had filed out.

"Excuse me, Professor Gram," I said softly, and she looked up at me.

"Yes, Kya."

"Can I speak with you about my grade?"

"I figured that you might want to discuss your grade," Professor Gram said and took off her glasses. Behind those thick black frames, she had soft pretty eyes. "We've talked about this before, Kya. I am just not seeing the quality of work coming from you that I am positive you are more than capable of producing."

"I know, and I'm trying, Professor Gram, but ..." I held up the paper. "It seems that I'm not getting it."

"No, you're not. Have you considered getting a tutor?"

"Yes, I've tried and none of them are accepting any more students." Professor Gram rattled off a few names of tutors, but I had tried them all. "Grad school at Massachusetts Institute of Technology is out if I can't get this grade up, Professor Gram."

She sighed deeply and then she looked up at me. "I'll tutor you, Kya," she said.

"Thank you, Professor Gram. I really appreciate you taking the time to do this," I said, as she wrote something on a piece of paper and handed it to me.

"That's my home address and phone number. Be there on Saturday at seven."

"In the morning?"

"No, at night," Professor Gram said, and began organizing her things to leave.

Even though I wasn't feeling doing this on a Saturday night, I wouldn't look a gift horse in the mouth, so I said, "Thank you, Professor Gram. I will see you Saturday night at seven."

"Please be on time, Kya. Punctuality is a sign of character," she said as she stood up, picked up her things and headed toward the door with me trailing behind her.

It was a little before seven o'clock on Saturday when I parked in front of the address that Professor Gram gave me and turned off the car. I got out and approached the house, which was cloaked in darkness, and made me wonder if she was home. I rang the bell and got no answer.

I walked back to my car thinking about her last words to me, *Please be on time, Kya. Punctuality is a sign of character*, and wondered what her lateness said about her character.

I was just about to get back in my car, when a silver Audi A7 came zooming down the street and pulled in the driveway. I looked at my watch and saw that it was six fifty-seven. Professor Gram got out of the car.

"Bet you thought that I was going to be late after I told you to be on time, didn't you, Kya?"

"Yes, I was just wondering what it said about your character," I said, and wished I hadn't. I was trying to get this woman to bump my grade up to a B, and here I was getting smart with her.

"And you would have every right to, because I got a bit carried away at the gym tonight. But ..." she pointed at the clock on the wall. "As you can see, I am on time."

"Yes, you are," I said, as she took off the jacket she was wearing. Prudish looking Professor Gram was rocking a two-piece workout suit. The black and orange sports bra cupped her full round tits. The spandex of the material showed all her curves. Especially in the pants that held her fat ass and round hips and the knot between her thick thighs. Who would have guessed it, Professor Gram was sexy.

She led me into the dining room. "This is where we'll be working, Kya, so make yourself comfortable. I'm going to take a quick shower and then we can get started."

When Professor Gram came back, she was wearing a long flowing caftan that came down to her ankles and I noticed that she had a butterfly tattoo on one. The material was the color of seaweed and sheer enough for me to almost make out the dark circles around her nipples. The slit in the front showed off her legs as she walked.

For the next two hours, Professor Gram gave me tips, pointers, and tools that I thought would really help me going forward in her class.

"I hope all that was helpful, Kya?"

"It really was, Professor Gram. Thank you so much for taking the time to work with me."

"It was my pleasure, Kya. You're a bright girl and you have a great future ahead of you. I just think that it is my job to push you to do your best work," she said, and stood up.

I stood up too. "Thank you, Professor Gram for caring enough to push me." I paused. "But there's just one more thing," I began.

"What's that?"

"The D I got on my last test."

"You want a chance to make it up, don't you?"

"Yes."

Professor Gram stood there with her hands on her hips and looked at me hard before she said, "I tell you what, Kya, you write me a paper on The Harlem Renaissance period and if you get an A on that, I will change that D to a B. Is that fair enough?"

"Yes," I said excitedly and threw my arms around her. "Thank you, Professor Gram. I promise to do a good job," I said with my arms still wrapped around her.

"I know that you will, Kya," she replied, but she still had her arms around me and I was beginning to think our contact had gone to a different level.

Professor Gram and I stood there in each other's arms, staring in one another's eyes. Her hardening nipples were pressed against mine. Her hand drifted down my back before she cupped and squeezed my ass. Before I could say anything, she pressed her soft lips against mine. My first time kissing a woman.

She caressed my ass, almost reverently and kissed me over and over, mumbling something about how inappropriate it was for us to be doing this, but she didn't stop kissing me and it damn sure didn't stop her from reaching under my dress, easing my wet thong to one side before penetrating me swiftly with two fingers.

"Professor Gram, do you really think we should do this?" I asked her, though I was sure I wanted to do it.

"Doesn't it feel good, Kya?" She touched my lips with care before patting on them as if to soothe my cat.

"Yes, it feels great."

"Do you want it to stop?"

"Hell no," I responded.

43

Before I knew it, Professor Gram had eased me down onto her dining room table, pulled off my thong and lifted my legs into the air. Her mouth hovered over me, the warmth of her breath making me shiver. Her tongue ran circles around my clit before taking it into her hot mouth.

As the professor sucked my bud, she slid two fingers inside my wetness and began rubbing my spot, making me arch and moan. I spread my legs wider so that she could gain better access, which she used to begin to attack me with flicks of her tongue and sweet suckles.

"Let's take this off," she lifted her head to say and I sat up to gather my dress, quickly pulling it over my head and then struggling to unhook my bra as Professor Gram attacked me again.

I laid there watching my beautiful English professor with her face buried between my thighs, her hair fanned out over her face and my legs. I was overwhelmed by the way she held my clit between the gap in her teeth and flicked it with her tongue.

I closed my eyes and squeezed my nipples as my essence began to flow; Professor Gram blew her hot breath on my clit. It sent a tingling sensation through my swollen clit that seemed to radiate throughout my body so quickly that I lost control and started to shake on top of the table.

"Oh shit!" I screamed. "I'm gonna cum!" I yelled and screamed my pleasure, as Professor Gram moaned and plunged her fingers deeper inside me.

I exploded and it felt like I was going to pass out, I came so hard. I sat there on her dining room table thinking that, except for me using Blackjack on myself, that she had just made me cum harder than anybody ever had. Professor

Gram helped me down from the table and led me to her bedroom.

"Have you ever been with a woman before, Kya?" She asked as we walked down a hallway.

"No," I said sheepishly. Mostly because my body was still trembling from the inside out and it kind of freaked me out that a woman could do that. I wasn't even into women.

"You are so hot, Kya, I'm surprised," she said.

Professor Gram brought me to her bedroom and we lay across her bed. She rolled on top of me, kissed my lips and then slid her body along mine; allowing our mounds to slide against each other and the tension began to build as we bumped harder and harder.

All I could do was moan at the sight of her sliding her body against mine. When she slid her nipples over mine, I nearly lost my mind. I began squeezing her tits, gently squeezing her nipples, and then I started kissing and licking her neck, sucking and gently biting on her earlobes.

When my index finger found her clit, Professor Gram's mouth opened in a loud sigh. She laid spread eagle across the bed, and I crawled between her thighs for my first attempt at eating pussy.

I've had mine licked and sucked enough, how hard could it be?

Let's just say practice would have to make perfect.

Professor Gram didn't move at first, as I ran my tongue long her smooth lips.

"Take your time, Kya," she said. "Use the tip of your tongue and flick it."

When I did as she instructed, her body trembled and she moaned out louder, spread her thighs in a way that said she wanted more.

"That's it. Now use the flat of your tongue and lick it like it's your favorite treat."

I opened the professor up with my tongue and was encouraged by her writhing on the sheets; I took her into my mouth while sliding two fingers inside of her.

The professor grabbed my head, and held it tight as the motion of my tongue against her clit intensified. I began fingering myself furiously, and she began slamming her face into my mouth. When I felt her clit getting hard, I knew she was no longer able to control herself.

"Yes, shit, yes!" she screamed, her face was twisted and contorted.

First Professor Gram tutored me in English, and then she tutored me on how to suck her pussy and make her cum.

DEEP

Study Hall

For the last couple of weeks, Ray and I were going through ... I don't know ... a funny stage. Well, truth is, there has never been a stage in our relationship that hasn't been funny; there just hasn't. There was a whole lot of sneaking to fuck, and neither of us had any business doing that, but neither of us seemed to care. So we snuck and fucked.

But like I said, over the last couple of weeks, things have been different, and the difference is, we haven't been fucking. I hadn't seen Ray since he fucked me at the Doubletree the last time I was home. It's not that I didn't want to see him, but I had to study and I didn't have time to drive home on the chance that he might have time for me. And when I asked Ray to come up here to see me, he'd always have something that he had to do with or for Mousy.

I was looking forward to seeing Ray this weekend, his dick to me was like the perfect remedy for anything that was bothering me. Right now, what was bothering me was writing this fucking paper on the Harlem Renaissance period. So instead of Ray having his dick inside of me, I was doing this shit, so that wasn't happening. When I called him to cancel, something he'd done with me countless times because of Mousy, he was a bit put off.

"What do you mean you can't make it back into the city? I got us a room."

"Just like I said. I have to get this paper back to Professor Gram by Monday morning so that she will at least bump me up two-letter grade so I can get a B. You have no idea what I had to do to convince her to give me this chance."

And he didn't. And he didn't need to.

That was the other reason that I hadn't exactly had time for Ray. I'd been at Angela's house just about every night this week. Being with a woman was everything I thought it might be.

Now, I know what you're thinking, and you'd only be half-right. Yes, we have been having sex. What am I saying, we've been having incredible ... no, amazing ... sex, but she's *actually* been tutoring me too.

We have sex afterwards.

I know that she's done tutoring for the night when she stands up and comes out of her clothes. I love the sight of Angela's rich brown skin when she's down on her knees, taking her time licking her way up to my pussy; starting from my toes, along my calves, and stopping between my thighs. The way she licks my lips and bites lightly on my clit always makes me even slicker with desire. Then she very deliberately spreads my lips with her fingers, and begins making small circles around my core with the tip of her tongue.

Even now, when I close my eyes, I can almost feel her tongue gliding along my flesh. Just thinking about it makes me want to grabbed Blackjack, set it on slow love, and play until my body quivers.

Don't get me wrong; I am not, by any means, complaining about having Angela share her pussy sucking skills. But no matter how many times I made her scream, she wasn't going to just give me an A. So, I had work to do.

"I'm not letting her bring down my GPA over some bullshit."

"I see. Well, I guess I'll see you next weekend then." And then he hung up.

I wanted to get into my feelings the way he seemed to have gotten into his, but I had a lot of work to do to get this paper right. So Ray would have to wait.

I was able to get six pages finished four hours later, but another four were needed before turning it in. But I was hungry, so I decided to go to The Shack. The place where you could buy food made on the grill and grab a sugary drink to keep you hyped enough to stay up late studying and, in my case, writing a paper.

But, to my surprise, when I pulled up at the curb of my building, there was Ray in his car.

"What are you doing here?" I asked him as soon as he stepped out looking so damn delicious. Ray had this thing about him. Deep penetrating eyes, smooth brown skin, the color of brewed coffee; baldhead, sexy lips, bowlegs, big feet and hands. If I wasn't still hot in the ass and trying to see the world, he might make me fall in love with him. But for now, he could give me the dick.

"I planned to taste your pussy all weekend, and I will. Is that cool with you?"

Just like that, I forgot about food and the paper and invited him up to my dorm room, but when he got there, he laid out some ground rules as I started to unbuckle his belt.

"Kya. Kya, look at me."

I looked up at him, but placed my hand on his hard dick, rubbing it up and down, paying special attention to the fat head that I could feel through the black denim.

"Yes?" I asked him, hoping he would hurry up with whatever lecture he was about to start.

"School is important, which is why I'm here to make sure I help you stay focused."

That made me laugh. "You being here doesn't help me stay focused at all, at least not on my paper. But on this ..." I stroked his hard dick again, my pussy was so swollen and dripping wet, I needed him to stop playing. "On this, I'm completely focused."

He didn't stop me as I squatted down in front of him, hurrying to reveal his dick to my eyes. When I freed him, he groaned out as if he was in pain.

"I'm going to take good care of it."

I took him into my already hot mouth, slobbering all over it in my haste to fit it in, which was always impossible, but I didn't give a damn.

The taste of his precum in the back of my throat made me hustle harder to make him nut. He palmed my head as I worked back and forth, squeezing his balls before placing them into my mouth and sucking gently on them as my hand continued to jerk him off. My spit was making the job easier.

In no time, he was ordering me, "Put it back in your mouth, Kya. Take this dick. Suck all that nut out."

And I did, loving the taste of his thick cum coating my throat.

"That's it, Kya. Swallow it all up."

I stood up, grinning at him before I sashayed over to the sink in my room. I started to brush my teeth and gargled with mouthwash while he just stood there with his hands on his hips, dick now semi-limp and hanging out of his jeans.

When I finished cleaning up, I asked him if he was all right.

"Yeah, I'm good. I'm just trying to figure out how I can help you finish this assignment so we can really start to have fun. That job you just gave me, Kya, made me want to say fuck it."

"Then I need to hurry up then."

Moments later, I was back in front of my computer and back to my paper when his voice interrupted me.

"What's the paper on anyway?"

"The Harlem Renaissance period. The professor said I didn't capture the essence of the struggle and the need for this movement in my first paper."

"Hmmmm," I heard Ray say. "I can help you with that."

I turned to him and had to blink a couple of times at the sight of him sprawled out on top of my twin-sized bed like a contented lion.

And yes, he was naked.

And yes, that dick was hard again.

All I could do was shake my head at this fine ass man.

"You can? How?"

"In college, we spent a lot of time studying The Harlem Renaissance period."

I just stared at him.

"Don't look so surprised, Lil Girl. I have other skills besides making you scream."

"Really?" I asked, because it intrigued me, and when I say that it intrigued me, it made me want to fuck him. So I came out of my chair and moved over to the bed. Now he was stroking his big black cock, so I leaned forward and swiped my tongue against his pebbled nipple just the way he liked it, before working my way over to the other one.

"Really? Tell me what you have so far."

I took his cock in my hand. "I know that during the nineteen twenties and the mid-thirties, Harlem was a literary, artistic, and intellectual movement that kindled a new black cultural identity."

"At the time, it was known as the 'New Negro Movement'." Ray laughed a little. "That's what we were called back then."

"I know that," I said, and tapped the head of his dick.

"But did you know that it was named after the nineteen twenty-five anthology by Alain Locke."

"I never even heard of Alain Locke. I just know that the movement included people like Langston Hughes, Countee Cullen and Zora Neale Hurston."

"Right. The white folks were fascinated by 'the exotic world of Harlem,'" he said, using air quotes before returning his hand to his dick. "So the publishing industry started publishing black writers that were focusing on realistic portrayals of black life." Ray squeezed the shaft and I watched as the plump head swelled, making my mouth water. "Now conservative black critics were afraid that ghetto realism would impede the cause of racial equality."

This shit was turning me the fuck on. Ray had been a walking-talking dick to me, but to find out, after all this time ... that he has a brain too ... I leaned forward and took him into my mouth. "I'm listening."

"Sure you are," Ray said, and reached behind me to undo the clasp that was holding my halter top up in the back; so now, my breasts were bare to his eyes. Ray quickly took my nipple into his mouth and sucked it hard. I pulled back just long enough to come out of the drenched coochie cutter shorts that I had been wearing around all day. His hand immediately went to my cunt. Ray gently slid his fingers around my slick pussy, making me gush even more.

"How about this," his voice rumbled as I started to move my lips around his navel and his thighs, before grabbing his heavy dick in between my palms, "I'll talk you through it."

"Like I said, I'm listening." I slid the head of his dick between my lips and kissed it before saying, "You were saying some shit about the movement impeding racial equality. And I started sucking him off as he continued the lesson.

"The intent of the movement wasn't political but aesthetic. So any benefit a burgeoning black contribution to literature might have in defraying racial prejudice was secondary to ..." He stopped for a moment to run his fingers through my hair and to guide my head up and down on his dick a little faster. "... As Langston Hughes put it, the expression of our individual dark-skinned selves."

His dick was wet with my spit; I took it into the palm of my hand and stroked it up and down on one side, while I ran my lips and tongue up and down the other side in a rhythm before taking it deep in my throat.

"That's it, work my dick, Kya."

I felt it swelling.

"The essence, that your professor might appreciate, was the life of the Negro was finally being expressed through art. We seized that opportunity and made it explode."

Interestingly enough, I think he was about to explode again, but he must not have wanted that.

"Get on your knees, Lil Girl, and place your hands on the headboard."

So much for the lesson, I thought as I did exactly as he wanted. I turned towards the head of my bed and held on to the headboard.

He was behind me in no time, sliding his fat cock inside of me, making me choke out, "Damn it, Ray. Give me that big dick!"

"That's right. Talk that shit to me."

He slammed into me ruthlessly and I did everything in my power not to be too loud. Even though it was a weekend and even though there were plenty of things happening on campus, there were other students on the floor and that included our nosey ass R.A. I didn't want to get kicked out of this dorm where I had a room to myself. So I squeaked out my moans and let Ray work himself in and out of my fat pussy.

"Damn, Lil Girl. Your pussy is so damn fat and wet."

That was it. I was cumming all over his dick, nearly hitting my head on the damn headboard over and over again, crying out his name as he held onto my hips and fed me that dick. When Ray reached between my thighs and fingered my already sensitive button, I began slamming my ass into him. My moans and cries began to get louder, so Ray pressed me down on the mattress and put his hand to my mouth to quiet me.

All I could do was hold on and suck on his finger, tasting my juices from earlier and enduring and enjoying this sweet torture. Ray took his hand away from my mouth to slap my ass, before he pressed my face into the mattress.

I began chanting quietly. "Fuck me, fuck me, fuck me."

Ray must have heard me because he picked up his pace.

I kept chanting, "Fuck me, fuck me, fuck me, Ray," and bounced my ass into him. That must have sent him over the cliff because Ray hurriedly pulled out of me and jerked his dick. But he wasn't done with me.

"Roll over and grab your ankles, Lil Girl," he demanded.

Yay! I said silently, because he was about to get all up in this pussy and I fucking loved that shit.

Ray leaned in and licked my slit, before he rose up on his arms and entered me slowly until it was so deep inside me that I thought I would feel him up in my stomach.

"I ... love ... getting ... this ... pussy," Ray said and paused and then rammed that big cock in me with each word. And then he gave it to me hard, deep, and continuous, just the way I liked until he pulled out of me and shot his hot cum all over my stomach.

We both lay there, looking at one another for, I don't know how long, panting and silent and unmoving until he said, "Go get cleaned up. I need to sneak down to the bathroom. I'll be back and you better be working on that paper. We need to get a room tonight. I'm definitely not done with you.

Three's Company

It was Friday afternoon and instead of going home, I decided to stay in our little college town for the weekend ... again. And I must be honest with you, a big part of that is Angela. Yes, it's Angela now.

"Somehow, Kya, I think that you still calling me Professor Gram is a little formal at this point, don't you think?" she asked me in bed one night after she made me cum for the second time.

And somehow, I couldn't disagree with her logic.

Ray went home that past Sunday night after he helped me rewrite my paper. He was a big help. As soon as he was gone, I printed the paper and went to Angela's house for her to read it.

"You couldn't wait until class on Monday to turn this in?" Angela asked me when she opened the door with her nipples pressing against a sheer white robe.

"No, I really couldn't."

I sat there quietly that night watching Angela while she read my paper. Every once in a while, she would smile, then she'd looked up at me and I took that to mean I had done a good job. I noticed something else too. Every once in a while, her nipples would get hard and press against the fabric.

What's up with that?

Anyway, once she finished reading it, she told me that I had written an excellent paper and had earned an A, and that I would get a B for the class. She paused. "Dependent on you passing your final, of course," Angela told me that night and to celebrate, she said that we were going to P.F.

56

Chang's for dinner. When she stood up and said she was going to get dressed, I just looked at her.

"What?" she asked when she saw the expression on my face.

"Do we have to leave right away?"

Anyway, like I said, Angela was a big part of the reason I was still in town.

Do you want to know why? Shit, I know you do.

After we got back from P.F. Chang's, Angela broke the strap out on my young ass and I nearly lost my fuckin' mind. You hear me, brains ... gone. I mean, she already had me screaming from her quick tongue and fingers, but the addition of that damn strap to her arsenal had me asking, "Can I come over tomorrow ... to study?" I was studying all right; my eyes were glued to her the entire time she was between my thighs.

But it wasn't all sex. Angela was serious about her tutoring me. She said that her being my tutor would require commitment on my part, so I was there every afternoon after my last class and she tutored me for two hours.

We'd have awesome sex afterwards.

But we talked too. She would talk about this other professor, she wouldn't reveal his name, with whom she had an affair, but he ended it when he started fucking one of his students.

Ironic?

Perhaps.

I wanted to know who it was, but since there were a few adjunct professors and I'm not an English major, it would have taken a lot of time and energy to figure out who was the one that had Professor Gram all heartbroken. Whether she'll admit to it or not, I figured his actions had to fuck her up for her to bring it up.

It was another Sunday afternoon and I had been at Angela's house all weekend and surprisingly, we hadn't opened our legs to each other yet that day. She had a thing about intellectual stimulation getting her off, which I could completely appreciate, so she'd been tutoring me for the final.

We'd been talking about literature from the Victorian period, and I could tell by the way she was talking that she was summarizing and we were about to move on to the more pleasurable part of the evening, when my phone rang. I thought it might be my dad, because he left me a message last night asking why I hadn't come home in the last couple of weeks.

What was I gonna say? I didn't come home daddy because I'm having tremendous sex with my English professor and by the way, one of your friends is fucking the shit out of me 'til the break of dawn?

I don't think so.

So I was avoiding any conversation with my dad until I was ready to tell him a lie. But thankfully, it wasn't my pops calling. When I looked at the display, it was Ray. I wondered how he'd found the time to call on a Sunday. Usually that day was off-limits, though there were times, as recently as last week, which he was with me on that day. He and Mousy usually were *cuddled* up together, or whatever the fuck they did when he wasn't fucking me or thinking about fucking me.

I looked at Angela, she smiled and motioned for me to answer it. "Hello?"

"Hey, what you doing?"

"Nothing, well, I'm over Professor Gram's house."

He was quiet and then asked, "She's the one tutoring you, right?"

"Yeah."

"I understand. That's important. So, I'll let you go so you can get your grade up," he said.

"Thanks for being so understanding, Ray, I'll call you tomorrow," I said, and he ended the call without saying anything else.

He sounded disappointed, and honestly as much fun as I was having with Angela, I really enjoyed Ray's dick in my pussy and in my mouth much more. I missed it. Since she was just about done, I could have easily told her that I had to go, but I wasn't about to play her like that. Not when she held my grade in her hands.

"Boyfriend?" She surprised me by asking.

"Kind of," I admitted.

I didn't want to get into logistics with her, because the one thing I always agreed to with Ray was that his status was no one's business. They didn't need to ever know he was married and since he wasn't a ring wearer, that wasn't a problem if he happened to be seen out with me. The reality was our age differences probably was the biggest problem, but neither of us gave a shit. I was old enough to not get him into trouble with the law and he fucked this young pussy like it was grown.

"You should invite him over then. I'm sure I can be a *gracious* hostess and make him feel welcome."

I looked at her with surprise. Was Angela trying to set up a threesome?

"That's if you're okay with it, Kya," she added.

She was serious, and I had to think about if I was okay with it.

Ray wasn't my man, not in the traditional sense anyway, but yeah, even though I had to share my dick with Mousy, I was a bit possessive about his dick. Mostly because of how good that shit made me feel. There were moments that even when we weren't fucking, I'd think about how cool we were together, but I was far from being in love.

I mean, Ray couldn't and didn't love me. Ray was fucking me, fucking me right, but to him, I was just some fine, young, wet pussy that he could get when he had time for it. I didn't need no dick, not even Ray's dick, taking up that much space in my heart.

But still, did I really want to complicate things for myself. You know what I'm saying? Like I said, bad enough I had to share my dick with Mousy, what if he wanted to come over here without me and fuck Angela? That might make me feel … I don't know … some kind of way for sure. But damn, all of this thinking was fucking me up.

"You can set whatever ground rules you like about just how gracious a hostess I should be, and then we go from there," she said, as if she was reading my mind. "How does that sound?"

"Okay. Let me call him back."

"You can step outside to make your call, if you like." Angela smiled at me the way she does when she's really hot and wet for me. "That way you'll have more privacy."

I stood up. "Be right back."

When I made it to the porch, I dialed his number and tried to think of how I was going to do this. He answered on the first ring.

"Yeah."

"You can stop through if you are game."

There was silence on the line.

"Game for what?"

"The professor ... well ... uh ... she said she would welcome you if you wanted to come through."

More silence.

"Why don't you go on and just say what you're trying not to say. I don't have time for these guessing games."

"You see, me and my professor, we're ... umm ..."

"Fucking. I know that. Shit, you're over there all the damn time, I'm not stupid enough to think y'all doing that damn much studying." Ray laughed hard. "What, she wants to do the group thing now?"

"Yes."

"I see. What she look like, Lil Girl? I'm not trying to fuck some old ugly white woman." Ray paused. "Unless it's the only way you're getting an A out the class," he kept laughing. "In that case, I'll come fuck her to death."

He had me laughing too. "No, Ray, nothing like that. Professor Gram is a sexy brown-skinned woman with a fat wet pussy."

"Well what do you want, Lil Girl? Are you down for this? I was hoping to check you out tonight. But if it's not a good time, we cool, it can wait."

"I'm cool with it, Ray, but the thing is ... I—"

"You have some rules. I promise I won't come back and bone your teacher without you. And we'll only do what you're good with. Cool?"

"Cool."

"Cool, give me the address. I'll be over as soon as I get some rubbers."

I gave Ray the address to put in his navigation system and then I went back in to wait for him to get there so both Angela and I could welcome him *graciously*. I was thinking that there was nothing wrong with a little bump and grind while we waited, but Angela poured us a glass of Chardonnay and we talked about Ray.

It was almost an hour and a half and a couple glasses of wine later when Ray called and said that he was outside. I went out to get him while Angela went in her bedroom to freshen up. Before we went in, Ray asked me if I was sure that I wanted to do this. "Yes. So come on, let's go."

When Ray and I walked in the house, Angela was standing there waiting for us. "You're Ray?" she asked, and looked like how I had been feeling about him for a year.

Yes, this man is fine and he's mine, so pick up your lip.

"Yes, and you are Professor Gram."

"Oh please, call me Angela. Let's have a seat."

We sat down, me closest to Ray with the professor in a chair across from us. We chitchatted for twenty minutes or so, and the entire time, Angela could not keep her eyes off Ray. We then got into a discussion about the Romanticism period in literature and when Ray told her that he majored in English in college, Angela was hanging on to his every word. She was smiling so hard, I thought her cheeks would break.

DEEP

I began thinking it was a mistake bringing Ray here. But at the same time, I was getting excited because I know how Angela had a thing about intellectual stimulation getting her off, and it was having the same effect on me.

After the Professor asked Ray if he had been tested recently and he said yes, she got up and came over to the couch and sat down on the other side of me. Ray smiled at me and so did Angela. She had now placed her warm hand on my thigh. I was wearing one of my casual T-shirt dresses, so it took only a quick move to have it pushed up my thighs and gathered in my lap.

It exposed my wet pink thong that was getting wetter as Ray started to tongue the skin behind my ear. His large hand palmed my breast, squeezing it at the tip of my nipple through the fabric, making me moan out.

Angela got up and quickly pushed her coffee table out of the way, dropped a pillow on the floor and was down on the floor pulling my thong to the side. She placed her finger against her clit and rubbed around it, making me arch into her and Angela smiled. She was really getting to know my body and how to touch me.

Ray was pulling my dress over my head and just as quickly, he had my bra off. Ray sucked on my tight nipples, and I reached out to grab his hard cock through his jeans. He unzipped his pants, took his dick out and stroked it for me as Angela spread my thighs wider. "I wanna taste you," she said.

I leaned over and took him into my mouth, as Angela proceeded to circle my clit with her hot wet tongue. She

63

flicked and swirled and sucked on it with just the right pressure.

I was in fucking ecstasy, you fuckin' hear me! I was deep throating Ray; he was guiding my head up and down and Angela was making my body tremble, sucking my clit, and licking it with the tip of her tongue.

I came so hard that I rushed to remove Ray from my mouth to keep from clamping down on him.

"I think we'd be more comfortable in the bedroom, don't you think?" Angela said, looking at Ray and held out her hand to him like she was his bitch.

But what came next shocked me.

At first, I thought he was going to take her hand but instead, Ray picked me up from the couch and while in his arms, kissed me. For one small moment, I thought, *does he care about me or something?* But as soon as he started to move us towards the bedroom following Angela, I came back to reality. This was about fucking.

When Ray placed me down on the bed, Angela immediately went to him. While I looked on, she undressed him and I began touching myself, eventually finger fucking my pussy to the sight of them undressing. He kissed her briefly, touched her skin in a way he didn't touch me, but still skillfully. Once she was completely out of the yellow sundress she was wearing, Ray leaned down and pressed Angela's tits together and started licking them as he gently squeezed them.

Then she kneeled in front of him and took him into her mouth. I watched spellbound at the sight of Angela rubbing and slapping her pussy while she sucked Ray off. He was looking at me and I got so fuckin' turned on that I began mimicking her movements, eventually cumming on my hand.

Even though Angela's mouth was full of his dick, Ray stepped back and Angela tried to reach for him again but instead, he came over to the bed and got between my thighs.

He started to kiss me here and there before attaching himself to my wetness. Angela got up from the floor and got in bed with us. As he licked me exactly the way I had grown to love, Ray turned on his side and Angela immediately took him back into her greedy mouth.

I sat up to watch as his dick disappeared into Angela's mouth. I listen to the slurping. Her sucking his cock, his sucking my cunt was so fucking hot and too much for me to hold on. I was screaming out again and squirting onto the sheets while holding onto my breasts.

"That's it, Lil Girl. Get that shit all over me," Ray shouted and his words made me squirt again and I screamed.

"Now come ride this dick," he ordered and looked at Angela. "You, I wanna taste."

As I positioned myself over him, Angela moved up to kneel over his mouth, but she was facing me. I impaled myself on that fat cock and started to rock my hips.

Angela exhaled when Ray first ran his tongue down her slit. When Ray nibbled on her clit, Angela and I kissed, and then she sucked my nipples as I rode him slowly. As he licked and sucked Angela's dripping wet pussy, he pushed himself as deep as he could inside of me. Ray made me cum, and Angela came right behind me.

We both rolled off of him and fell out on either side of Ray, he was still rock hard. He began kissing Angela, and I started stroking his dick and squeezing his balls, before I took him into my hungry mouth. Angela got up on her knees and crawled over to me. She began running her hands over my body, starting from my ankle, then rubbed along my leg until she reached the wetness between my thighs.

Then Ray moved my head and looked at Angela.

"Come here. I wanna fuck you now." Ray got up, grabbed a rubber from the bed and slid it on. He walked around the bed, pulled Angela's ass up and slammed his dick into her.

"Your dick is so big and hard," she cried out, and then buried her head between my slick thighs again.

I lay there in complete ecstasy, while Angela worked magic with her tongue and watching Ray slam his body into hers, while she squeezed my nipples and feasted on me.

Then Ray pulled completely out of Angela, stroked that cock a few times and then he slammed himself into her again. When he was inside her, Ray smacked her ass as hard as he could.

"That's it." Ray spanked that ass again. "I like it like that," she moaned, and stuck two of her fingers in her mouth and moistened them before she slid them inside me and zoned in on my G-spot.

"I know you like that, don't you, Lil Girl?" she asked, looking in my eyes.

Her calling me Lil Girl the way Ray does when he fucks me got my river flowing. Angela had me dripping wet as usual. I closed my eyes and started thrusting myself onto her hand and I drenched Angela's fingers with my juices.

I looked at Ray, his eyes were closed, and he was pumping away. After a few more hard strokes, Ray pulled out of her and sprayed his hot cum on her cheeks. When he was done, Angela quickly spun around, pulled the condom and took Ray into her mouth.

I watched, gently massaging my swollen lips, while Angela sucked and stroked him. Once his dick was firm again, she turned around, put his dick back inside her, and dropped her head back between my thighs.

Angela licked me with the tip of her tongue and when she slid her tongue inside of me, and sucked my clit until it grew harder, my body began to quiver and I screamed!

"Oooh shit! I'm about to fuckin' cum again."

Ray pulled out of Angela again. "Roll over and lie on your back." He looked at me. "Sit on her face so she can make you cum again, Lil Girl," he ordered and we both did what he demanded.

I gently bounced my pussy on her face and I felt my nipples stiffen as I watched Ray fuck Angela. When Ray spanked her thigh, and said, "Stop fuckin' around and throw me that pussy," the sensation turned me on. The sound of him sliding in and out of her made me wetter.

Ray grabbed her by the hips, and pulled her body into his. She started twisting her hips, and throwing that ass at him the way he demanded. "That's it, Teach, get this dick." He looked up at me. "She got good pussy too, Lil Girl, but not as good as yours. Ain't that right, Teach," he said, and fucked her hard and she screamed out her orgasm.

I had been with Ray long enough to know that when he picked up his pace that he was close to cumming and I wanted his cum in my mouth, so I made my move to get it. Ray smiled because he knew what I wanted.

"You want this cum, Lil Girl, don't you?"

"Yes," I pleaded. "Give it to me!"

When he pulled out of Angela and pulled off the rubber, he grabbed my face with both of his hands, stuck his cock in my mouth and coated my throat with his hot cum.

Yeah, this was the shit.

DEEP

Moving On

This had been an amazing school year. That's what I was thinking as I packed up my things and waited for my parents to come up to help me move back home for the summer.

I had an internship at an engineering firm to keep me busy, but I also had so many memories of my time with Ray, Donny, Angela, and a few others that I didn't tell you about. You know, those club hookups I mentioned.

I ended things with Donny like I said I would. I got tired of all the sneaking around behind my best friend's back.

More about that in a minute.

But when Tiana caught Donny with another friend of ours named Candice, she finally started believing what I was trying to tell her about him.

Now, let me tell you about my best friend. I came home one weekend and since Mousy decided to reel Ray in a bit more, I called Tiana. "Hey, girl, what's up?"

"I'm into something right now, Kya. I'll call you back."

An hour later, Tiana calls me back and says that she got a room at the Marriott and says come through. "And bring your stuff in case we decide to go to Club Passion."

I'm like, "Cool," and Tiana gives me the room number. So we're sitting there, smoking, laughing, doing shots of Patrón, and the liquor had Tiana talking. And I mean, she was telling all her business. I thought about telling her about Ray but I knew I never could or would betray him and sharing that would betray him...us. So I told her all about me and Angela.

"I didn't know you were into women."

"I wasn't. It just happened," I said, and even though she didn't ask, I told her about all that too and we drained the bottle. We stopped drinking, but I didn't stop talking. After a while, I had a rush of conscience and started to tell her about me and Donny and hoped that our friendship could stand it.

But before I could get it out, Tiana starts talking about getting out of there and going to the club, bounces up and starts looking for something to wear. Since I'm a little tipsy, I say that I'm going to jump in the shower first to wake up. I get up, get undressed and head for the shower. I might have been in there for five minutes when the door creaks open.

"Can I get in with you?" Tiana says to me, standing there naked. I admit she had a nice body. She tells me that she's always been into women, but since I wasn't, she never came at me that way. "I ain't in love with you or nothing like that," she added as she pulled back the shower curtain and stepped in under the spray with me. "I've always wanted to suck on those big juicy tits."

"But you're my best friend," I protested mildly as she began to fondle my breasts, her fingers tracing my nipples as she began to lean forward.

"Now we'll be better friends," Tiana said, before taking my hard nipple into her hot mouth. So there was that.

Then there was Angela. She wasn't too happy when I told her that I had an internship lined up. She was making plans for us to go to Europe for the summer and although I hated to pass up that opportunity, I thought working toward my future was more important than speaking French while fucking her all summer.

Anyway, I ended up acing the final and getting an A in her class. After a good bit of pleading on my part, Angela allowed me to do a makeup project. "That and one other thing, Kya." She wanted me to bring Ray over so he could fuck her in the ass while I masturbated in front of her. The things we do to maintain our GPA.

But in that, I found out something about myself. Now that I had my woman experience, which was great by the way, I really did love dick better. Which brings me to Ray.

As far as Ray was concerned, he and I hadn't been going at it like we used to after that last time with Angela. I was spending a lot of my time studying. I did have other classes, you know, and since I wasn't fucking my other professors, I needed to study for their finals. Even though I always wanted to see Ray, he wasn't always available and by the time he was able to get back to me, there wasn't time to actually do anything or sometimes I was already preoccupied. Plus, Ray didn't like me not being available when he was, so I wouldn't be surprised if he had some other woman's legs up and I had a feeling that it wouldn't be long before Ray found his way to Angela's door. Ray's not the type of man to stop just because I wasn't available. And I was sure that she would welcome him graciously. Even more so, now that she wouldn't have to compete with a younger better pussy.

She got good pussy too, Lil Girl, but not as good as yours. Ain't that right, Teach? I will never forget him saying that as long as I live.

So, as much as I liked some good dick, sometimes it wasn't worth all the trouble. One day there will be a man with a heart that I will love and he can give me all of him. He just needs to have a big dick and eat pussy like it's his last meal.

There was a knock and my father pushed open my door bringing in a dolly with him. Behind him was a man so damn fine, that school, my future, my internship, all that shit was a distant memory; just that quickly.

"Hi, Babygirl," my daddy said. "Let me introduce you to Carlos. He will be working in my shop this summer and I asked him to help me get you back home."

My father was talking about how my mom was downstairs talking to some of the other parents and how he was glad Carlos came with him because as usual, I had too much stuff for him to move by himself, but my attention was squarely on the golden-skinned Carlos. This would be a great summer.

Kya Returns In:

The Kya Chronicles

Office Intern

Here's a Sample:

THE KYA CHRONICLES

Office Intern

DEEP

DEEP

THE KYA CHRONICLES

Office Intern
By Deep

©Deep 2017

Wet N Deep Publishing

NAUGHTY GIRL

The Good Girl

What was it about a fine black man in a suit and tie that made my pussy clench?

I mean, it couldn't just be any shirt and tie, seeing that suits and ties were all I spent my time around these days. At Morgan, Tesson and Associates, the dress code was always professional with the exception of the company's casual Fridays that most didn't observe and so us, the summer interns, didn't either.

Joshua Macklin was the department's director. Age thirty-nine, well over six feet tall, low-cut hair, neatly trimmed beard, and fuckin sexy. The interns never had a reason to have much contact with him since Shannon McDonough did the supervising of interns but today I had been called in to speak with him about the project I just completed. Which was why I was wondering how I would keep my fast ass seated instead of jumping onto his lap to ride him.

"Kya Garner, 3.8 GPA, active member of Sigma Eta Xi, entering your senior year at the University of Chester. Quite impressive, Ms. Garner."

"I'm glad I can impress you, Mr. Macklin."

"Call me Josh, Kya, please. Everyone else does around here," he said, relaxing back into his black leather executive chair. A chair big enough to hold us both up if only he'd allow me to show him.

"If it's okay with you, sir, I'd rather not. I respect people in positions of authority. Call me a good girl ... in that regard."

He stared at me for a while, his dark bedroom eyes quickly shifting to my crossed thighs before returning to zero in on my warm face. Though I really wanted to unbutton my blouse just to cool off and to give him something to really fucking look at, I resisted and remained well behaved.

For now.

"A good girl, huh?" He chuckled, but those eyes shifted to my cherry painted lips.

"Yes, sir. I know how to be good at everything I do. Which is why I'm so glad to be working *under* you, sir. I feel I will do my very best work with you to guide me through each and every step. Don't you, sir?"

I watched as he shifted in his seat, the only sign that my words might be having any effect on him at all.

"I believe you're right, Ms. Garner. Shannon mentioned that your insight into the Microfiltration Project was masterful. I thought maybe you needed to advance ahead of your peers for the remainder of the summer."

"Thank you, Mr. Macklin."

"You have another four weeks in the program and due to me shifting some work to George in his new role as Project Manager, it's freed up a bit of my time. So, I'll be able to work with the brightest star on our team of associates … one-on-one."

My pulse was racing, my heart was thumping inside of my chest, I bit my bottom lip out of excitement, not at all anxiety.

This was perfect.

"That is if you'd be interested, Kya," he went on to add.

Hell yeah I was interested in any and all one-on-ones with this fine man.

"The opportunity sounds too perfect to pass up. I'm all yours for the next four weeks, sir."

"Good girl."

Damn.

I really wish we could get started right away.

But be a good girl, Kya.

Over the next couple of weeks, I was a good girl; stayed out of trouble, did the work that was assigned to me and – if you can believe it – I kept my legs closed. Trust me, that one wasn't easy. There were many afternoons when I was glad that I got to the store so Carlos could fuck me in the warehouse while he was on break. But even though his cock was big and he had some idea of how to use it, it did little to curb my lust to ride Mr. Joshua Macklin in that black leather chair.

After a long day of juggling the few assignments that Shannon placed on my desk, because apparently, she felt I needed more work to do all of a sudden. I was able to meet with Joshua in his office for our one-on-one; my favorite part of the day.

After yesterday's close call, I was wondering if he'd find an excuse to cancel this meeting and I had even been so bold to send him an email asking, "Are we still on?"

To which he replied, "If I cancel, you'd know."

That only made me more wet and anxious to have our meeting. I didn't care if he only planned to show me the specs for the project he was overseeing in the Champaign District. If I had to just sit there and look at him while he talked, it would be more than enough to get me so slick that the moment I got to my car, I'd place my foot upon the dashboard and commence to fucking myself with my Blackjack travel companion.

He could hold out as long as he wanted because his voice got me off. Even if I wanted to swallow his dick whole, and wished to taste his salty cum, I'd settle for that smooth baritone any day.

I waited for everyone else to leave the floor, irritated when Shannon came to my cube to ask how long I planned to stay over. I told her that I was still working on one of the things she placed on my desk an hour ago, though honestly, I had finished, but it gave her a reason to shut up and go. Good, I needed to get with Josh.

I hustled to his corner office, happy that not another soul was around to see me going in his office, that way maybe he'd let himself go like he did last time. Laughing with me in a way that was not reserved for his other employees.

This I was sure of.

I knocked on his cracked door and his deep voice reached out to me and said, "Come in."

When I walked into his office, for some reason today, it seemed smaller, more consumed by the man sitting at his desk, holding his phone to his ear. He gestured for me to sit, his expression serious and focused on the words pushed out of the receiver.

I sat in the seat directly in front of his desk and situated my notebook on my lap before crossing my legs. When I looked up, his eyes were fastened on them with such intensity that I knew he would rather look at my legs rather than continuing his phone conversation.

His eyes moved to mine and the burning look he gave me confirmed my thoughts.

Without a word, I uncrossed my legs, allowing enough of a gap between my thighs for him to see that I was bare beneath my skirt, my pussy slick and wanting. Gauging his reaction, I shifted, crossing my legs again and waited to see what would happen next.

"Larry," he said quickly. "All of that sounds great and I think we're now at the stage where we can have our face to face. I'll have some specs drawn up for your approval and have Sally call you to schedule a meeting."

His eyes went back to mine, and with a pull that I had not even experienced with Ray, I was drawn to wanting to please this man. The tips of my tits were rock hard beneath my bra, my hands shaking from the need to reach out to him to put us both out of our misery.

But this was my internship, not something I planned to fuck up, so I'd have to wait this out until he made it clear that I could have his dick.

And I wanted his dick badly.

The thought of gagging on it – just once – made my pussy cream and threatened to have me leaving a wet spot on this chair. It was torture knowing that he wanted to fuck me as much as I wanted to fuck him. But due to professional lines, that most companies thought were important and I thought was ludicrous, you ended up with a whole bunch of horny muthafuckas that are angry and frustrated all day. So, we had to pretend that screwing each other wasn't what this was all about. These one-on-ones now only served one purpose. They allowed us time to mind fuck each other.

Sure, I learned a few things. He was brilliant but the fact was, the sight of his big ass hands moving the mouse around on his desk only had me thinking about him fingering me, making me squirt on top of his desk and him lapping that shit up. His long legs that he had to stretch out every so often, forcing him to get up and pace around as we talked, only made me think of riding those hard ass thighs, bouncing my pussy up and down his thick hard pole.

And when he licked his lips to moisten them, I wanted to take one into my mouth and suck on it before devouring his mouth while he pounded into me.

I sat watching him, watching me and he ended the call right as I was about to give up my fight of remaining a good girl and just set this pussy out in front of him so that he had to take it.

"Ms. Garner," he finally acknowledged me.

"Please, call me Kya, Mr. Macklin. Everyone else does around here."

It was a familiar rejoinder that only got a half smile out of him. He seemed bothered which made me wonder if I had pushed too far with letting him see this creamy hot pussy a moment ago.

"We have another two weeks to work together, Ms. Garner."

"That's correct, sir."

That's why I was so at the point of begging him to fuck me since I knew it would be over soon and I'd be back to school, hoping some good dick came along.

And yes, I do mean Ray ... whenever he had time.

"Would you say you've gotten what you need here at Morgan, Tesson and Associates — that you've learned a great deal in this internship?"

"Well of course, Mr. Macklin. My time with you has been the most valuable. I wouldn't otherwise know about driving force, retentate and permeate streams. I don't regret a moment of it," and pinning him with my stare, I added, "Not one moment."

He got up from his chair then and started his usual pacing only this time, the print of his hard dick was evident. It pressed against his zipper as if it insisted I take him out and believe me, I wanted to.

Kya be a good girl.

But why the hell would he do this shit to me? Tempting me this way.

"I'm glad to hear it. Really glad."

He turned from his big window and glanced down at my legs again and I opened them wide enough that there would be no doubt that I was ready whenever he was but instead of taking the bait, he turned back to the downtown skyline.

"I pride myself on being able to spend time with the brightest among us, helping to cultivate them into the young engineers that will one day shape our future. It's important that they get the guidance they need," he was saying.

And while he went into some of the projects he saw come out of the engineers he directly tutored; of its own volition, my hand crept in between my thighs. I couldn't help it. His voice always had me at this place where screwing was the only thing I could think about. Where having his cock down my throat was the only image I could see.

I started to rub myself, spreading my juice all around my pussy and rubbing circles around my now hard clit when I heard, "Ms. Garner."

Shocked as if I had forgotten he could see me, my hand stilled. I had gotten so into it, the heel of my shoe was now up on his desk, giving him a clear view of my fingers working my pussy.

"I'm so sorry, Mr. Macklin," I said, though I wasn't, but I was afraid he'd kick me out of the program.

He walked over to stand in front of me where I was still as stone. My hand still against my throbbing wet cunt.

"Don't be sorry, Ms. Garner. I understand. Can't you see that?"

Nodding, I waited, avoiding looking at the hard package directly in front of me.

"My priority was to make sure you had the proper guidance from me. So that you can go into your senior year more ready than before."

"I understand that, sir."

"Do you, Ms. Garner?"

"Yes, you needed to get the important things out of the way first."

"Exactly. And now that they are ..." my breath caught in my throat as I waited for him to continue, "We can continue with other matters over the next two weeks, Kya. That is, if you want to?"

"Oh yes, Mr. Macklin. I told you I'm a good girl. Just tell me when it will be okay to proceed."

He stared at me, his jaws were clinched, and his gaze burning with fire. He was on the edge just as I was and we needed to just fall over the edge together.

"Take it out, Kya," he ordered me and without a blink, I was hurrying to unbuckle his trousers, and fumbling with his zipper before pulling them down along with his silk boxers.

I gasped when his cock was in front of me with no barrier. Perfection was the only way to describe it. It was long and thick, gorgeous brown-chocolate, and hard.

With my eyes, I tore my attention away from this glory and looked at him, pleading with him to release him from his agony and he responded by saying, "Be a good girl, Kya."

I pulled him into my mouth, gag reflexes be damned, and tried to get him to nestle near my tonsils as I explored the taste of him.

As I drew back, I savored the taste of the sweet pre-cum at the tip, which I lavished with kisses from my soft lips. He reached out and grabbed my head, his fingers running through my hair before cradling my skull with care. As I worked back and forth, making sure to get his dick wet with my spit, he guided me back and forth on his length, gagging.

I went back to rubbing my pussy, so close to cumming just from this blowjob, I slowed the rubbing to hold it off. He pulled back some, letting me adjust before shoving it back in, and chanting, "Take it, Kya. Be a good girl."

So I took it and as a reward, those magnificent fingers of his replaced mine as he leaned down to take over. I sucked his dick and he rubbed my pussy. He petted that muthafucka, making her purr, before penetrating me with two of his thick fingers. I scooted up so that he could get deeper which made him tell me to stand up.

He unbuttoned my blouse and cupped my tits in his big palms before leaning forward to suckle on each hard nipple. He licked and laved them, and made them so hard that they hurt before pulling back and helping me out of my skirt. Now I was naked in his office, living out the fantasy I had for more than a month. He walked over to the door and made sure it was locked, something I should have thought about long ago, and started to undress in front of me.

When I reached out to help him with his shirt's buttons, he pushed my hands away and told me to, "Lie back on my desk."

I moved a few things aside, jumped up on the desk, and leaned back on my elbows so that I could continue to watch him as he came out of his shoes and took his pants and undergarments all the way off.

If I had known this man looked like this under his clothes every day, I would have been kicked out of this internship long ago. I would have snuck into his office sooner, waiting beneath his desk so that when he sat down, I could attack him and suck his dick while he told me to stop, eventually shutting up as I forced him to cum.

Damn.

He reached into his pants pocket and retrieved a rubber out of his wallet, stretching it over his still glistening cock.

He came to me and leaned forward, kissing me gently before devouring me. We moaned in each other's mouths, only pulling apart to breathe. His kisses over my bare skin did little to calm me, they only inflamed me as they reached my stomach where he licked around my naval. I watched him kneel in front of the desk, his eyes directly in front of my pussy. His fingers came up to open my fat lips before he pulled me into his mouth.

The texture of his smooth lips and his warm tongue flicking against my bud, made my hips come up off the desk. He placed his hand against my hips to hold me in place as he used his other hand to begin fingering me. His fingers stretched me as they moved in and out of me, his lips attached to my core, made me seize upon his desk.

I yelled out, "Fuck, I'm gonna cum," and instead of pulling away, he kept on going, forcing me to cum in his mouth.

I was so sensitive and needed him to stop but he didn't. I tried pulling away but he wasn't having it.

He murmured, "Be a good girl, Kya, and take it," and I exploded again, only this time I squirted from the intensity.

Now pleased, my body still twitching where I lay, I was focused on breathing. He stood up and licked my juices from his lips, while he moved between my thighs and spread them apart and back so that my knees were pressed to my chest and then he slid into me slowly.

"Oh shit," I moaned. "Damn!"

"Fuck," he bit out before pulling out and slamming back in. "This pussy feels good wrapped around my dick."

"Mr. Macklin!"

His thrusts were well paced. Steady, hard, and deep. My body moved back and forth on top of the desk as he held my hips so that I could take each pump.

The sounds of my wet pussy popping and his thighs hitting my skin and the desk made it sound like construction was happening. And maybe it was because I certainly was being demolished and something else was being built inside of me again. This orgasm was so large, so heavy that I was afraid of it.

Him chanting, "Good pussy from this good girl," had my pussy grabbing and releasing his dick like it was afraid of losing him, and I couldn't hold back anymore when he pressed his finger right against my clit.

It was impossible not to scream out, "Mr. Macklin!"

He just kept pummeling my G-spot; hitting it over and over and making me cum again and he was clutching me so hard that it hurt, but I didn't give a shit.

"Take this pussy ... yes!"

"Damn, Kya. Fuck!" And then he was jerking and losing his rhythm and beat and fucking me so hard that all I could do was hold on for fear of us both collapsing on the desk.

Breathing heavy, he leaned up and kissed my lips before pulling out. I lay there panting and shaken to my core by how powerful that shit was. If I didn't watch it, this man would turn me out.

"We can't do this here again. You're a screamer and I love that shit."

NAUGHTY GIRL

Made in the USA
Middletown, DE
15 February 2017